THE SANDTIGER

BY JENNY HAMLETT

ILLUSTRATED BY JANE TATTERSFIELD

Chapter 1

Peter drew a tiger in the sand. It was huge. It had pebble eyes as big as oranges. It had paws like plates.

Peter worked hard on his tiger. He worked all afternoon. He found some driftwood and gave it whiskers. He drew a bowl of spaghetti so it would

have something to eat.

His twin sister Susie came to look.

"What on earth's that?" she said.

"It's my Sandtiger."

Susie laughed.

"It eats people who laugh at it," said Peter crossly.

"It won't have time," said Susie.

"Why not?"

"Look at the sea," she said. Peter looked. The tide was coming in. Soon the waves would be lapping at

the tiger's paws. The beautiful Sandtiger would be gone, lost forever under the cold slimy water. Peter ran straight to his Mum.

"The sea won't come up any more, will it?" he said.

"Why yes, love," Mum answered. "It's only half way up now. The high tide comes all the way to the bank I'm sitting on." Peter tried not to cry but the tears came by themselves.

"What is it?" Mum asked.

"My Sandtiger's going to be drowned," Peter whispered.

"Let's go and have a look at him," Mum said. Peter followed Mum to where the tiger lay on the sand with the sea just touching its toes.

"What lovely stripes," said Mum cheerfully. Peter said nothing.

"I do like the sandy squiggles. What are they?"

"Spaghetti, of course," said Peter.

Mum tried again. "Beautiful big eyes."

"I found his eyes over there." Peter pointed to some rocks where he'd found the two shiny pebbles. Mum took his hand and squeezed it gently.

"Such a magnificent tiger couldn't just disappear," she said. "Look at him. He's caught in the sand now, but when the sea covers him the tiger will be free to swim away underwater."

"Do you really think so?" Peter looked down. The Sandtiger did seem as though he were getting ready for a swim.

"I'm sure of it," said Mum.

"I bet it won't," said Susie. "That's just a made up story."

"Nonsense," said Mum quickly. "Time we were getting back to tea." She began to pack up the beach things, the spades and buckets, boots and coats but not swimming costumes. It was Easter and still too early in the year to swim. Peter ran quickly, picked up a handful of pebbles and put them down beside the tiger. He could eat them when the spaghetti ran out. He would need his strength. His toes were disappearing.

"Come on," said Mum, "scones for tea." Peter's Mum was one of those people who always tried to make the best of things.

"We've got jam and cream today," she said. She went first, carrying the bags, up the steep path that climbed to the top of the cliff.

Peter went last but he didn't look back. He hoped and hoped that Mum was right about the Sandtiger. Perhaps he would swim away underwater? Peter was afraid that if he looked back he would break the spell and see the tiger washed away for ever. So, he looked straight in front of him all the time, all the way up the cliff.

Chapter 2

After tea Peter went upstairs to the room he shared with Susie. She was there already, sprawled on the bed with her Lego set. She looked up as Peter came in.

"Don't touch it," she warned.

"I wouldn't want to," said Peter. He flung himself down on the bed with a book but he didn't read it.

"Susie?"

"Quiet, I'm thinking."

So Peter was quiet. He lay on his stomach with the book open in front of him and his eyes closed. Perhaps the Sandtiger would come alive after dark? No, not completely in the dark, in the moonlight. Peter imagined a huge yellow moon with the face of a Sandtiger rising over the cliffs.

He would go down to the beach by the light of the moon. He wouldn't be frightened of the dark because the moonlight would be his friend.

The sand would be empty but he would sit and wait until he caught a glimpse of a dark shape moving far out ...

"You don't believe in all that stuff Mum told you?" asked Susie. Peter's eyes flew open.

"What stuff?" he said.

"You know, about the tiger. You don't believe it'll really swim away."

"Yes I do."

"You're just daft," Susie sneered.

"I'm not."

For the hundredth time Peter wished he didn't have to share a room with Susie. It was lovely to be on holiday but the house wasn't big enough. What chance did he have of dreaming about the Sandtiger with Susie butting in all the time? If only the tiger was real. That would show Susie. She wouldn't be laughing then. If only the tiger could come alive. If even now he was just coming out of the sea and wading through the shallow water to get to the beach. If ...

CHAPTER 3

The next day it was pouring. Rain rattled on the corrugated iron roof of the garden shed and washed across the cliffs in sheets. There were lumps of grey mist moving over the sea like monsters and the fog siren was sounding. It made a deep, unhappy booming at regular intervals as Peter stood looking out of the window. It was just the right sort of day for a Sandtiger to slip across the sand and creep quietly up the cliff. He would come knocking softly at the back door and give a low growl which only Peter would understand. But Mum wanted to go to the museum.

"It's a horrid day," she said. "Let's go and visit something."

"Oh no," said Peter, "I don't mind the beach in the rain."

"You'll catch a chill down there in this weather," said Mum.

Susie said, "I wonder if it's the sort of museum that has skeletons?"

"I don't want to go," said Peter. "I don't like skeletons. They're boring."

"Come on," said Mum, "we must do something." She went out to the hall to get the coats.

"Hurry or we'll miss the bus."

They just caught it. They were the only people on it. As they sat watching the rain beat against the windows the driver chatted to them. He put them down right next to Trevent museum.

"Although what you want to go there for," he said, "beats me. Nothing there now but musty old relics. Not worth wasting ten minutes on, let alone a morning."

"Oh dear," said Mum when he'd gone, "I hope he's wrong."

The museum was worse than expected. It wasn't a modern museum with interesting buttons to press and lights that flash on and off. It was an old fashioned, dusty museum with the exhibits all jumbled up. The first room was full of grubby pots and pans. Mum tried hard to help them enjoy it.

"Your Gran used to use one of those," she said. "It's a griddle pan."

"What's it for?" Peter asked.

"To hit Grandpa over the head with," said Susie. Mum laughed.

"No," she said, "to cook scones on."

Peter looked at the dusty flat black circle of metal. He didn't fancy eating anything off it.

"Can't we go on?" he said. Mum looked down at him.

"You are bored, aren't you? she said. "Come on then. Let's go to the bird and animal gallery." She led the way into a long thin room full of glass cases. From the moment Peter put a foot inside the gallery he hated it.

The room was full of prisoners. From their glass cages their dead eyes stared. They seemed to watch his every move. Mum bent down in front of one of the cases.

"Peter, look at this. It's a Puffin," she said. "Isn't he beautiful?"

But the eyes were all around Peter, glaring, unfriendly. He hung back. He tried to think of the Sandtiger instead. Perhaps the tiger would come and rescue him and they would gallop off out of the museum, Peter riding on his back. They would be half way home before Mum and Susie could turn round.

Peter stood behind the Puffin case waiting, but the Sandtiger didn't come and the eyes were closing in. Suddenly he couldn't stand it any more. He turned and wandered away from Mum and Susie all the way between the glass cases and out of the gallery.

In the next room it was dark compared with the glass-roofed gallery and it was some time before Peter's eyes became used to it. At first he couldn't see anything at all but then gradually he began to make out a big leather sofa at one side of the room. Peter was just about to sit down, when on the floor beside it, he saw something else. He stood still. The something else wasn't even in a glass case.

It was difficult to see exactly what it was but he was almost, yes very nearly certain, it had wriggled. If it hadn't been for the eyes in the gallery he'd

have run straight back to Mum. As it was he stayed frozen to the spot staring at the strange thing. Nothing happened for a whole minute. Peter grew braver.

"Hello," he said. The creature did not answer.

"Are you alive?" There was no reply. Nervously Peter took a step closer.

"Can you hear me?" There was no movement from beside the sofa at all. He must have been mistaken. It was just another stuffed animal. Perhaps it had been chucked out the back because it was no good. Then suddenly he felt sorry for it. He'd almost decided to pat it when he heard Mum call. "Peter are you all right?" Mum sounded anxious and Peter turned back into the gallery.

"Let's look round the town," Mum said. None of them wanted to stay in the museum any longer.

As soon as they'd gone the creature in the small dark room blinked. It got up and shook the dust off itself. Then it padded softly out of the museum following quietly behind them.

Chapter 4

It was late when they got back, almost tea time. Everyone was tired and cross and hungry. Mum was busy with the cooking, rushing here and there in the kitchen so Peter got out of the way. He ran into the hall and was just about to go upstairs but Susie had taken over the bedroom as usual. He could hear her tapes through the ceiling. There was nowhere peaceful except the garden.

Peter wandered aimlessly across the lawn wondering what to do. It would be dark soon and then he would have to go back inside again. He noticed the shed door was open. That was odd. It had been shut ever since they'd come. The twins kept their bikes in the garage next to the house.

"How did that come to be open?" said Peter. He spoke aloud but there was no one there. He was talking to himself.

"First sign of madness, so they say," said a deep voice from inside the shed. Peter jumped.

"Who's there?"

"It's me."

"Who's me?"

"You know," said the voice, rather irritated now, "you drew me. I've been following you about all day." Peter put his head cautiously round the shed door.

"Was it you in the museum?" he whispered.

"Yes."

"Why didn't you say something?"

"Because the others might have heard of course."

Peter slipped inside the shed but stayed close to the door. Lying on the floor in front of him he could just make out a huge stripy tiger. It lifted its head and looked straight at him. He hesitated.

"Come in. Come in. Don't be shy. I won't eat you," the tiger said and laughed.

"Are you really the tiger I drew?"

"Of course I am!" The Sandtiger stood up and shook himself.

"I'm starving," he said. Peter's heart pounded. Supposing the Sandtiger was dangerous. Supposing he was only pretending to be friendly and was really going to eat Peter as soon as he came close enough. He stepped back a pace. The Sandtiger seemed to know exactly what Peter was thinking.

"It's all right," he said, "I won't eat you. I don't eat people. They're the wrong colour."

"Oh," said Peter.

"Well come on in then." Suddenly brave, Peter went straight up to the Sandtiger and stroked his neck. The tiger licked Peter's hand.

"If only there was something to eat in here," he sighed.

"Oh dear. What do you like to eat?" Peter asked. He was still rather nervous in case the tiger changed his mind and said people, but he didn't.

"I don't eat anything in the dark," he said sadly.

"Why not?"

"There are no colours in the dark. Everything turns to blacks and greys so I have to wait for daylight."

"Pardon?"

"I only eat yellow."

"What?"

"Oh I eat anything that's yellow. I'm not fussy."

Peter stood staring at him in surprise but the Sandtiger lay down again and made himself comfortable. It was as though he had something very important to say and must be in the right position to say it.

"I was born under the sea," he began dreamily, "but there was nothing to eat. It was all green weed and black rocks. By swimming and wading, I found my way on to the land, but that wasn't any better. The fields were full of more green grass and

then came the town, all grey roads, pavements and houses. It was a nightmare and that museum was the worst of all, full of browns and purples."

"What did you do?" asked Peter, anxiously.

"Oh, I got a bit of a snack in the park."

"Yes?"

"Yes, a baby dropped a yellow rattle and I gobbled it up quick before his mother had seen it fall."

"Didn't the baby mind?"

"I don't think so. He was crying but he started to laugh when he saw me eat it. It didn't go far though. I was still hungry. It was only a snack after all."

"There's some yellow straw behind the shed," Peter said helpfully.

"Won't do me any good until morning. I can't see it. But thanks for telling me anyway." The Sandtiger yawned and settled down to sleep.

"Good night then," said Peter. There was no answer but a loud snore.

Chapter 5

Peter woke early, very early. He could hear the cock crow from the farm across the road. His stomach was full of excitement and he couldn't wait to get out to the shed. Susie woke up just as he was putting his clothes on.

"Where are you off to in such a hurry?" she said.

"Wouldn't you like to know?" Peter laughed and dragged his socks on as quickly as he could. Susie was more awake now. She pulled herself up on to her elbow.

"Well go on. Tell me."

"I won't." Peter ran off down the stairs leaving Susie looking after him. Puzzled.

The early morning was still misty and very quiet. For one awful moment Peter thought he had made the whole thing up. Perhaps he had imagined the tiger last night? But as he walked down the path beside the lawn he heard the comforting sound of loud munching coming from behind the shed. The Sandtiger looked up as he appeared.

"Not bad for an early breakfast," he said with his mouth full of straw. "I'll take my main breakfast in half an hour."

"Isn't the straw enough then?"

"I'm a growing animal," said the tiger. "I need sustenance."

"What does that mean?" asked Peter.

"It means," said the Sandtiger very firmly, "that I need plenty to eat. Sandtigers cannot live by straw alone. We must have a balanced diet."

"Oh." Peter began to wonder whether a Sandtiger might not be a rather difficult pet.

"We'll have to ask Mum for some yellow things she doesn't want," he said.

"You'd better not," said the Sandtiger hastily.

"Why not?"

"Because I'm a secret. If you tell a secret, it's not a secret any more."

"But then how are we going to find you something to eat?" asked Peter. The Sandtiger took a deep breath and blew out his chest.

"We must forage, like explorers," he said. "It'll be hard work but well worth the effort."

"I think there are some daffodils on the compost heap," said Peter doubtfully. "Mum threw them out but they're still yellow."

"Lead the way," said the tiger.

They went across the rough part of the garden behind the shed. Little curls of mist still hid the houses on the other side of the lane. No one was about. The long dewy grass wrapped itself round Peter's legs and made his socks damp. But the Sandtiger liked the wet. He pranced about in it.

"It's like a shallow sea," he said. He enjoyed the daffodils too but he didn't find them filling. He sighed.

"I suppose I can just about hold on until it's time for my mid-morning snack," he said. "I shall go and have a lie down in the shed to conserve my strength."

"I'm not certain but I think we might go to the beach this morning," said Peter, and then more anxiously, "Do you think you'll be all right?"

"Of course I will. Don't you worry about me," said the tiger. "I'll be fine."

Chapter 6

The beach was lovely, sparkling in the sunlight and the tide was out. They built a monster castle with a ditch round it. Peter ran in the wind across the flat sand and tried to fill his bucket with water without getting his jeans wet. He almost forgot the Sandtiger. He completely forgot about the tiger's mid-morning snack until Mum called, "Time for a biscuit."

With a horrid sinking feeling in his stomach he wondered just what the tiger had found to eat.

"Let's go back now," he said. Mum was surprised.

"Go back? But we've only just come!" Peter tried to think of a good reason for wanting to go home.

"I don't feel very well," he said.

"Hum," said Mum, "you certainly look a bit peaky. Perhaps we had better get back then."

"Oh," Susie groaned, "I haven't built the ramparts yet."

"It can't be helped, love," said Mum. "If Peter's not well, we'll have to go."

"Trust him!" Susie said and stomped off to get her spade. They were back well before lunch time but it was not soon enough. The washing-up bowl which Mum had left outside to dry had disappeared.

"Has one of you taken it?" asked Mum.

"Not me," said Susie. Peter shook his head.

"Well, where can it have gone then?" She went to look for it in the kitchen. Peter didn't follow. He crept quietly down to the end of the garden on his own. The washing-up bowl had been yellow.

The Sandtiger was waiting for him in the doorway of the shed.

"I must have some lunch," he said. "At once!"

"But you've only just had the washing-up bowl," said Peter. The tiger smiled. "Very tasty too but I need something a little more substantial."

"More straw?"

"No that blows you up, but it isn't satisfying."

Peter sighed. By now he had decided that it

would definitely be better if the Sandtiger continued to be a secret. What Mum didn't know she couldn't get cross about.

"Well come on," he said. "We'll go and look. You don't want to be seen though, do you? You'd better go carefully."

"I'm always careful," said the tiger. Peter went out of the shed first. The Sandtiger followed on tiptoe.

"I'll be as quiet as a mouse," he said.

This time they went beyond the garden. Perhaps the lane or the cliffs had something yellow on them? But it didn't look too hopeful. They went past a row of back gardens, full of green plants. The daffodils were over and there wasn't anything else yellow in sight.

Number Twelve, however, had washing pegged on the line. There were jumpers and skirts and trousers, socks and shirts and underpants all blowing about in the wind. At the end of the line there were also two huge yellow sheets billowing like sails.

Peter and the Sandtiger caught sight of them at the same moment. The Sandtiger gave a yelp of delight. Peter flung himself on the tiger's neck, clutching him desperately.

"No," he shouted but it was too late.

The Sandtiger shook himself free and, like an arrow from a bow, he hurled himself straight at the sheets. There were a few moments of delicious chomping. Then there was nothing left but some shreds of tattered yellow, flapping forlornly from the pegs. Peter covered his eyes with his hands. What on earth was he going to do? The Sandtiger burped happily. "That's better," he said.

"But what about that lady's sheets?" Peter said.

"Oh, will she mind?" asked the Sandtiger looking surprised.

"Of course she'll mind. She'll be furious."

"Well at least you can tell her they were eaten in a good cause," said the Sandtiger.

"What good cause?"

"Me!" The Sandtiger drew himself up to his full height and purred.

"My stomach," he said.

CHAPTER 7

Mum was busy when Peter got back. She was hanging out the towels. Susie's was yellow.

"Mum," said Peter.

"Yes, love?"

"Mum, why not hang that yellow one up inside?" Peter said. Mum looked surprised.

"Why?" she asked.

"Well, wouldn't it dry quicker inside?"

"Possibly but it would drip all over the floor."

"We could put a newspaper underneath it," said Peter eagerly. Mum looked down at Peter, her face very puzzled.

"Are you all right," she asked, "or are you still feeling ill?"

"I'm all right, really, but please don't hang that yellow towel outside." Mum now began to look very anxious.

"I think you must have caught the sun," she said.

"You'd best go and lie down for a bit."

Peter didn't want to lie down. He was worried about what the Sandtiger would get up to when it came to teatime. Sandtigers obviously needed to eat very regularly. They needed an early morning breakfast, a main breakfast, a mid-morning snack and lunch. Very probably they would need tea, supper and a pre-dark, goodnight drink as well! It was coming up to tea time and Peter couldn't bear to think what might happen.

"Oh Mum do I have to lie down?" he said.

"Very definitely yes. You're looking white."

"That's worrying about the Sandtiger," Peter thought. He gave up trying to persuade Mum that he was better and went upstairs. But he could not lie down.

The Sandtiger may want to be a secret but somehow Peter couldn't see him staying that way for long. He stared out of the window hoping the tiger would stay safely out of sight in the dark shed. He was terrified his Mum would look up and see something large and stripy tip-toeing stealthily towards the yellow towel.

Peter went over in his mind all the possible and impossible diets that might suit a Sandtiger. More straw perhaps, but he probably wouldn't bother with that. There were a few dandelions already out on the lawn. They might keep him busy for a bit but not for long. Peter racked his brains to think of something else that was yellow but there really was nothing. He was sure that the yellow towel would be gobbled up. There just didn't seem to be anything else.

As it turned out Peter was wrong. The towel survived but Susie's beautiful new bicycle didn't. They both had racers, presents from Mum on their birthday just before they came away. Peter's frame was red and Susie's was bright blue. The bicycles had silver wheels but Mum had bought packets of beads and fitted them on to the spokes. There was green for Peter and yellow for Susie. When she cycled the beads made little flashes of yellow like small suns. They caught everyone's eye. Even stationary they caught the Sandtiger's eye.

"Yum. Tasty," he said and sidled up to the bicycle

while no one was looking. He opened his jaws wide and crunch went his teeth into the front wheel.

"Ugh!" The tiger got a mouthful of silver spokes as well and didn't like it at all. He spat most of it out but it was too late. The bicycle was ruined. The front wheel was hopelessly bent.

Chapter 8

"What horrible beast did this?" Susie shouted. Mum rushed out.

"Oh Susie, I'm so sorry. I can't think how it happened." Peter watched it all from upstairs. He knew he should tell Mum about the tiger but it all seemed to get worse and worse and he couldn't. Susie had started to cry. Mum hugged her.

"Never mind, love. We can get a new wheel. It'll be all right."

"It's been eaten," Susie sobbed.

"I can't think what can have done it," Mum said. "What on earth would want to eat a bicycle wheel?"

"It doesn't make sense," said Susie. "It's silly."

"Well come on. Let's have tea. We'll think where we can get another wheel tomorrow," Mum said soothingly.

Tea wasn't a very happy meal. Susie still kept bursting into tears and Mum kept trying to find ways to cheer her up but they didn't work. Nobody noticed Peter which was just as well. Peter was worrying and worrying about the tiger. What could be done about him? Eventually he would be discovered. What would happen then? Peter didn't dare think about it.

In the middle of tea there was a knock at the door. It wasn't a gentle 'I've got all the time in the world' sort of knock but more of a furious, hasty, 'let me in at once' bang. Peter ran to the door. But before he could turn the handle it burst open, nearly knocking him over, as Mrs Brant from across the road fell into the room.

"Quick," she said, "my dog's terrified!" Nobody answered her. They didn't know what to say. Mrs Brant struggled to her feet.

"Come on," she shouted, "you must call that huge cat of yours off."

"But we haven't got a cat," said Mum.

"Well what's that then?" screamed Mrs Brant. She pointed up the road with a shaking hand. "If I didn't know any better I would say it was trying to eat my poor Sandy for tea."

"I don't know what it can be!" said Mum. They all crowded into the doorway. A beautiful golden retriever was tearing up and down the lane as fast as it could go with its tail between its legs. After it, snapping his jaws with delight and lashing his long tail, bounded the Sandtiger.

"Oh no," Peter groaned. Mum looked down at him suspiciously but she said nothing. Then all the worst things that could happen, happened at once. The dog, seeing a way of escape, tore past them and on up the stairs. They could hear it bumping into the furniture and crashing about in the bedroom.

The Sandtiger was following closely behind but when he caught sight of Peter he stopped. Peter glared, hoping the tiger would get the message and go away. But he didn't. He gave a loud purr and came right up to Peter and rubbed himself against the boy's legs.

"I'm sorry," he whispered. "I got carried away." Peter couldn't help but smile. Mrs Brant saw it and came on like a live volcano.

"Do you mean to tell me you've been hiding that thing?" she shrieked.

"Well ... not exactly," said Peter.

"What do you mean not exactly?" Mrs Brant spat out.

"Peter!" said Mum in the voice she used when she wanted to sound cross. Susie began to giggle. By this time Mrs Brant's volcano was erupting.

"You keep dangerous pets and let them do just what they like. It shouldn't be allowed."

"He's not a dangerous pet," said Peter quietly. "He's a Sandtiger."

"I don't care what he is. There must be a law against it." The Sandtiger let out a low growl and moved towards Mrs Brant baring his teeth. She backed away. "It should be restrained," she said. "You must put it on a lead."

"We'll try not to let it happen again," said Mum hastily. But Mrs Brant had already started to fumble in her pocket, looking for some string. That was unfortunate. The Sandtiger thought she was looking for food. Suddenly he bounded towards her putting his paws on her shoulders and licking her

face. That did it. Mrs Brant screamed like a steam whistle, "Get this lang spider off me. No this tang slider. No this land glider. Oh, get RID OF IT!!"

Mum hovered about trying to calm things down, Susie doubled up with laughter and the dog still crashed around upstairs. Peter was the only one who noticed the woman from Number Twelve. She stood in the open doorway holding the remains of two yellow sheets in her hand. She just stood there watching. She said nothing. Then after several minutes of uproar she spoke in a loud clear voice.

"It must be put down," she said. Everything went quiet. Even the Sandtiger seemed to realise that something terrible had been said. He got down from Mrs Brant and slunk behind Peter, making himself as small as possible. Mum's face had gone quite white and Susie stopped laughing. Peter knew what it meant. The Sandtiger would be killed. He put his arm round the tiger's neck and held him close. Mrs Brant stopped screaming.

"That's a very good idea," she said. That was the last thing Peter heard. He turned and ran out of the door dragging the Sandtiger with him, not that the tiger needed much dragging. They both ran as fast as they could across the garden and towards the path at the top of the cliff. They didn't pause, even for breath, until they'd stumbled all the way down it to the beach.

CHAPTER 9

"What are we going to do?" Peter said.

"Don't know," said the Sandtiger.

"You have mucked things up."

"I'm sorry," he said, "but I was so hungry I didn't know what to do with myself."

"Are you sure?" Peter asked suspiciously. "You looked as though you were having a good time to me."

"Well yes. That too," the tiger admitted. "But I must feed the inner tiger you know."

Peter stroked him. "We'll have to find you something to eat that doesn't cause so much fuss," he said. "What about grass?"

"It's green," groaned the tiger.

"Well, insects then. There are some yellow ones I think."

"Ugh!"

"I thought tigers liked meat," Peter said.

"I wouldn't have minded that dog, if I could have caught him."

"Thank goodness you didn't. We're in enough trouble already."

The Sandtiger looked confused. "But we haven't done anything," he said.

"You don't realise," Peter said, "they want to have you put down."

"What do you mean, 'put down'?" asked the tiger. "Is it edible?"

"No, it means they want to have you killed."

"What!" The tiger leapt at least three feet into the air and began to bound off over the pebbles like a huge beach ball.

"Come on," he shouted. "There's not a moment to lose. We must get away."

"Wait!" Peter called out as he struggled after the tiger, slipping and sliding on the pebbles. But the Sandtiger would not wait. The bay was huge and seemed to stretch for miles and miles with the Sandtiger disappearing into the distance. Then for no reason at all he slowed down just as though someone had stuck a pin in him and all the air had come out. He went slower and slower until at last he flopped down on to the pebbles, panting. Peter caught him up.

"Come on," he said, tugging at the tiger.

"I can't."

"You've got to. They'll find us."

"I can't."

"Why not?" Peter asked.

"I'm dying."

"What?"

"I'm dying!" the tiger said louder as though he thought Peter might be deaf.

"Don't be silly," said Peter. "Of course you're not dying."

"I tell you I am. I'm dying of hunger."

"Oh no!" Peter sank down on the pebbles beside him. "What am I going to do with you?"

The Sandtiger didn't reply. He lay still with his head on his paws, the very picture of a beaten animal. Peter played with some pebbles by his hand. He fiddled with them as people do on beaches. He tried to think what he could do to get the tiger on his feet again.

As Peter thought he began to fling the pebbles towards the sea without really noticing what he was doing.

Each pebble sailed high in the air. They made beautiful curves, shining in the late afternoon sun. Then they landed splosh, splosh into the water. Without warning the tiger suddenly sat up, all alert. He stretched out his neck and caught a creamy coloured pebble between his teeth. There was the sound of crunching and swallowing.

"Yum. Lovely," he said. "Almost as good as yellow." He caught another and another. Then Peter was laughing too much to throw any more so he made a pile of them for the tiger to eat

They went down very well, even faster than a tin of humbugs he and Susie had once shared. At last the Sandtiger stopped.

"I can't eat anymore," he said. "I'm full. I'm really full."

"Hooray!" shouted Peter and his voice echoed against the cliffs.

CHAPTER 10

In the silence that followed they heard a cry, "Peter. Is that you?"

Peter and the tiger stared at each other.

"Where are you?"

"Shush," said the Sandtiger.

It was Mum of course. They both lay still behind a rock, holding their breath.

"She mustn't find you," whispered Peter.

"Quiet," the tiger whispered back.

They could hear the sound of feet coming across the pebbles. Mum called out again, "Peter. Where are you, love?" and then again more desperately, "Peter. Are you all right?"

Peter peeped round the rock. Susie was with Mum but the other two women weren't there. He watched them look everywhere, under the cliffs, behind the rocks.

He wanted to get up and run to Mum shouting, "Here I am. Don't worry." But the Sandtiger put his paw on Peter's arm and shook his head.

"I must tell her where I am," Peter said.

"It's all right for you," said the tiger. "You're not going to be killed."

"I'm sorry," said Peter and he lay down again. Mum and Susie had begun to climb over the huge stretch of black rocks in the middle of the bay. They were very slippery. Although Susie moved quite quickly, Mum could hardly struggle up the steep slopes. Peter watched as they climbed to the top of one rock and stood staring around them. Then it happened.

"Ah!" Susie cried out as she slipped. She fell, skidding down the whole side of the huge rock and vanishing into a crevice between two others. She didn't reappear. Peter was on his feet at once.

"She's hurt," he said. He saw Mum climb slowly down towards Susie and disappear too. They were gone for so long that Peter knew there was something wrong. He turned towards the Sandtiger.

"We must go and help," he said.

"Too dangerous. She shouldn't have come," said the Sandtiger unsympathetically.

She was only looking for me," Peter said. "Please help."

"No I can't."

"I'm sure Mum doesn't want you put down," said Peter hopefully.

"Hum!" The Sandtiger was obviously unconvinced. Peter wondered what on earth he could do. He couldn't leave Mum and Susie struggling on their own. Supposing Susie was badly hurt? Then out of the blue he had a brilliant idea.

"They may be hungry," he said.

"What?" The Sandtiger sat up immediately.

"Suppose they need something to eat," Peter pressed on.

"If Susie's stuck down there, she might starve to death." The tiger's face was grey with horror.

"We must help," he said. "They can't be left to starve." He stood up and galloped towards the rocks.

"Don't stand about wasting time," he called back to Peter. "They won't be able to hold out for long."

They both struggled over the slippery rocks. Peter

was very slow. In fact once or twice the tiger had to stop and lower his tail over a particularly high rock so Peter could use it to pull himself up. The Sandtiger wasn't pleased at all.

"You've been eating too much," he said. "You're as heavy as lead." At last they reached the dip in the rocks where Susie seemed to be standing awkwardly with one foot stuck out in front of her. Mum was bending down, trying to pull her leg. She looked so relieved to see them.

"Oh Peter. Thank goodness you're all right. Susie's foot is stuck."

Peter scrambled down the rock. His sister's foot was trapped in a little crevice. He knelt down and tugged at the rock but nothing happened.

"We must take your plimsoll off," Mum said. She tried to get the lace undone but it didn't make any difference. Susie still couldn't move her foot at all.

"I don't know what to do," said Mum. "She can't stay here all night. She didn't even eat any tea." On the magic words, 'She didn't even eat any tea' the Sandtiger sprang into action. He bounded forward and took a large bite out of the black rock.

"Ugh! Nasty black stuff," he said and spat it out as fast as he could. Then he bent down and took another bite.

Susie leant back away from the tiger as far as she could. "Is he dangerous?"

Peter began to understand what the tiger was doing.

"No," he said. "Keep still. It won't take him long."

The rock was beginning to break loose. For a moment, the Sandtiger paused to take a deep breath then, like a pneumatic drill, he attacked the rock again. He bit and spat and bit and spat so fast that Peter could hardly see what was going on. One last enormous bite and Susie's foot was free but she'd twisted it and she couldn't stand on it.

"She still can't get home," said Mum.

The Sandtiger lay down beside her, nodding his head to show he wanted Susie to climb on him. Cautiously, Susie lifted her leg over his back and sat down.

She wobbled as he stood up and clutched the fur on the back of his neck, but she seemed to settle down as the Sandtiger set off over the rocks easily and quickly. Mum and Peter were left, trying to keep up as best they could.

"Hope she'll be all right," Mum said.

"Course she will," said Peter.

As they came back down on the level beach Mum asked, "But where did he come from?"

"You know, Mum," Peter said. "You told me he would swim away under the sea."

"But that was just to cheer you up."

"Well, that's just what happened, only the tiger didn't like eating seaweed so he came out to look for us."

"Oh dear!" said Mum.

"He gets very hungry," said Peter.

"I had noticed," said Mum.

"He's very nice though," said Peter anxiously and then in a rush he said, "I'm afraid Sandtigers eat all the wrong things."

Mum laughed. "Well lots of us do that," she said. "Look at you and Susie. You'd live on crisps and Mars bars if I'd let you."

"You won't let them have the tiger put down will you?" Peter asked quietly.

"Of course not," said Mum. "We must find him something to eat though."

"He likes the pebbles on the beach."

Mum smiled. "That's a good start," she said. "We'll see what can be done."

CHAPTER 11

Susie and the Sandtiger were waiting at the top of the cliff. She was just offering her second yellow sock to the tiger. They both looked up guiltily as Mum and Peter appeared.

"I'm sorry," said the tiger, rather indistinctly through a mouthful of sock, "I just can't control myself."

Susie said quickly, "They were only old socks. They had at least two holes in them."

Mum laughed. "Never mind," she said, "I have some lovely old yellow dusters he can have for supper."

The Sandtiger gave a loud purr. But the dusters didn't turn out to be very successful. Mum, Peter and Susie all had cheese on toast for supper so the Sandtiger would feel at home. He ate a dozen or so slices and approved of them.

"A delicacy," he said, "but not a main meal of course." He then looked hungrily round for a second course and Mum hunted in the cupboard

under the sink for the dusters. It is true they were a bit grubby and a bit fluffy but ... the Sandtiger gulped them down. His face began to turn bright green.

"Help," he cried, "help, help." For one awful moment Peter thought the tiger was going to be sick but Mum patted him on the back quite hard.

"I think it's indigestion," she said. She patted him again and he let out a huge belch.

"Oh that's better," he said with a sigh of relief. "What do they put in those things?" He paced up and down the kitchen.

"Oh dear, oh dear, this rich food doesn't agree with me," he said. "I must stick to health foods in future."

"Do you mean the pebbles?" Peter asked.

The tiger nodded his head vigorously. "I think I'll go back down to the beach and have a snack," he said and he was off.

The tiger didn't come back to live in the shed. There was a nice dry cave down on the beach, handy for food.

"It's just as well," Mum said. "We can't take him back to London with us." But while their holiday lasted, Peter visited him everyday and Susie went too, when her foot was better. The tiger was obviously enjoying the pebbles.

"They keep me fit," he said.

He found room for Peter's titbits too. Bananas were his favourite. The skins, of course, were best although he managed to eat the insides as well. The tiger became rather anxious when it was time for Peter to go back to London.

"We'll come back in the summer," Peter said.

"I'm afraid my diet will be very restricted until then," the tiger sighed. So Peter collected up all the old yellow clothes that he and Susie did not need any more or thought they could do without. There were two jumpers and a bright yellow tee-shirt and another pair of socks. Susie wasn't sure about the socks.

"I might want them."

"Don't be mean," Peter said. Mum had the best idea. She cut up an old yellow sleeping bag.

"Well, I expect we can find the money for another one," she said. They took all these things down to the cave and stacked them at the back in a neat pile.

"Just have one now and again," Peter said firmly.

"You're not to eat them all at once." But the tiger looked at the pile longingly.

"Lovely," he said and licked his lips.

There was one small problem. The tiger ate so many pebbles that the creamy coloured ones on the beaches of north Cornwall became scarce. He thought of moving to the south coast but he decided not to when he heard that there were no proper caves there.

So he stayed in Cornwall. Sometimes he still had to forage when pebbles were in short supply. An odd tea towel would go missing from a washing line or a pair of yellow knickers but people thought they'd been blown away in the wind. It couldn't be helped, for a growing Sandtiger has to keep his strength up.